KU-175-746

In A Minute

For Stella, Toni and Biko
E.B.

For Anna
T.B.

Listed in *School Librarian's* top 100 titles for 1990.

"a model of what children's books should be in the 1990s."
School Librarian

Other stories about Jo and her family

Through My Window
Wait and See

In a Minute

Tony Bradman and Eileen Browne

"I'm ready!" said Jo.
She was going to the park
with her mum and dad.

Best of all, she was going to the playground
with its swings, see-saw and slide.
Sita and her dog, Patch, were coming too.

"Can we go now?" asked Jo.
But Mum and Dad were very slow.
"We'll be with you in a minute," they said.

Soon Mum and Dad were ready.
They went next door for Sita.

"Come in," called Sita's mum.

She was putting something in a bag.

Sita was looking for Patch's lead.
"Be with you in a minute," she said.

Now Sita was ready.

They set off for the bus-stop.
But on the way, Dad met one of his friends.

They stopped to chat.
"Dad!" said Jo. "We'll miss the bus!"
"I'll be with you in a minute," said Dad.
He kept on talking.

They missed the bus.

"Oh well," said Mum.
"There will be another one along . . ."
"In a minute!" said Jo.
But they had to wait for ages.

At last, they arrived
at the park.

They were just going in
when Mum met one of *her* friends.

So they stopped for another chat,
and to look in the buggy.
"Mum, can we go in now?" asked Jo.
"In a minute, Jo," said her mum.

They went into the park.
"This way to the playground!"
said Jo and Sita.

But Mum and Dad stopped to listen
to a woman making a speech.

Jo tugged her dad's arm.
"We'll be with you in a minute," said Dad.

They walked on and came to the duckpond.
Jo could see the playground
in the distance.

"Let's feed the ducks," said Mum.

Jo wanted to run on.
"Stay with us, Jo," said Mum.
"We'll be with you in a minute."

They left the duckpond
and walked towards the playground.

But then a carnival procession came by
and they stopped to listen
to the steel band.

"We'll never get to the playground," said Jo.
"Yes we will," said Dad.
"We'll be there in a minute."

At last they were at the playground!
Jo and Sita ran in through the gate.
But something terrible had happened.

The swings were tied in knots.
The see-saw was broken
and the slide had chains round it.

"It's not fair," cried Jo.

Suddenly Patch ran off.
"Quick, after her!" shouted Mum.
Jo and Sita chased Patch round the corner.
What do you think they found?

A fantastic new playground!

"Wow!" said Jo.
"Brilliant!" said Sita.
There were four bright red swings,

a stripy see-saw
and a great big elephant slide.

Jo and Sita swung . . .

and bounced . . .

and slid . . .
until they were tired.

Then they all sat in the shade
and had a picnic.

"Come on you two," said Mum and Dad.
"It's time to go home."
Can you guess what Jo and Sita said?

That's right!
"We'll be with you . . . IN A MINUTE!"